KT-435-715

Robyn
the Christmas Party Fairy

The Fairies wish Emilia a Merry Christmas!

Special thanks
to Rachel Elliot

ORCHARD BOOKS
338 Euston Road, London NW1 3BH
Orchard Books Australia
Level 17/207 Kent Street, Sydney, NSW 2000
A Paperback Original

First published in 2013 by Orchard Books

© 2013 Rainbow Magic Limited.
A HIT Entertainment company. Rainbow Magic
is a trademark of Rainbow Magic Limited.
Reg. U.S. Pat. & Tm. Off. And other countries.

Illustrations © Orchard Books 2013

A CIP catalogue record for this book is available
from the British Library.

ISBN 978 1 40832 791 3

3 5 7 9 10 8 6 4

Printed in Great Britain

The paper and board used in this paperback are natural recyclable
products made from wood grown in sustainable forests. The
manufacturing processes conform to the environmental regulations
of the country of origin.

Orchard Books is a division of Hachette Children's Books,
an Hachette UK company

www.hachette.co.uk

Robyn
the Christmas Party Fairy

by Daisy Meadows

ORCHARD

www.rainbowmagic.co.uk

The Fairyland Palace

Barn
Elf's Cottage

Clock Tower

Kirsty's House

Wetherbury Village

Jack Frost's Ice Castle

Hall

The High St.

Jack Frost's Spell

Come goblins all from far and near.
It's time to spoil their Christmas cheer.
Instead of parties, games and fun,
Bring tears and sighs to everyone!

The fairies and their human friends
Think that they can make amends.
But Christmas parties all shall be
Filled with despair and misery!

The Magical Cracker

Contents

Crazy Crackers

"I've never seen frost looking so beautiful," said Rachel Walker, looking out of the Town Hall window.

"It's a perfect Christmas Eve morning," agreed her best friend Kirsty Tate, joining Rachel at the window.

The bright winter sun was making everything outside the window glitter.

Kirsty's home town, Wetherbury, looked as if it had been frosted with white icing. The girls were spending Christmas together there, with their families.

"The party tonight is going to be amazing." Rachel smiled. "And helping to organise it makes it even more fun."

She turned around and looked at the busy preparations that were going on in the hall. Lots of people from the community had come together to put on a special Christmas party. The girls and their families were really excited. Everyone had made something delicious to eat, and the highlight of the party was going to be a performance of a famous ballet.

Mrs Tate saw the girls over by the window and smiled at them.

"Come on, you two, there's work to be done!" she said. "We've got a lot to do before the party. Could you start by laying the tables for the feast?"

Several long tables had been pushed together to make a big square in the centre of the hall. Mrs Tate gave the girls a trolley piled high with tablecloths, placemats, serviettes, cutlery and glasses.

"Don't forget to put a Christmas cracker on each place setting," she said. "The crackers are in a box on the bottom of the trolley."

"I'm so excited about the Christmas party," said Rachel. "Just think, people all over the world are doing exactly the same thing as us right now, getting ready for Christmas."

"Not everyone!" said Kirsty. "At school we've been learning about other holiday traditions from around the world, like Diwali and Hanukkah, and how people celebrate Christmas in different countries."

The girls worked quickly, laying out the bright red tablecloths and beautiful place settings. Soon the tables looked very Christmassy, with gold serviettes and sparkling glasses and cutlery.

"Just one more thing to do," said Rachel, peering into the box. "A cracker for each party guest!"

As she picked up one of the crackers, it gave a loud bang. Rachel squealed and dropped it.

"What's the matter?" cried Mrs Tate, hurrying over to the girls. "What happened?"

"I'm OK, I was just surprised," said Rachel. "This cracker went bang all by itself!"

"Oh dear, how strange," said Mrs Tate, taking the cracker. "I'm sure it must be faulty."

Suddenly there was another small bang
from inside the box.

"I've never known crackers to go off
by themselves before." Kristy frowned.

Mrs Tate opened her mouth to reply,
but then one of the other volunteers gave
a loud groan.

"This tinsel isn't sparkly at all!" she
said, holding up a long string of golden
tinsel. "It's just dull. We can't use it!"

"These decorations won't stay up, Mrs Tate," called another volunteer from up a ladder. "It doesn't seem to matter how many drawing pins I use, they just fall down."

Mrs Tate gave a heavy sigh and hurried off to deal with the new problems.

"Maybe I can see what's wrong," said Rachel, as she picked up the faulty cracker. She peered into one end of it like a telescope and gave a little gasp. A beautiful little fairy was sitting cross-legged inside!

A Banned Band

The fairy waved at Rachel and then zoomed out of the other end of the cracker. She was wearing a shimmering raspberry-coloured party dress and a thin golden band in her hair.

"Hello," she said. "I'm Robyn the Christmas Party Fairy."

"Hello, Robyn!" said the girls together.

"We should hide," added Rachel. "Quick, under here!"

The girls slipped under one of the party tables. The long tablecloth hid them completely.

"It's great to meet you, Robyn," said Kirsty. "But what are you doing here in Wetherbury?"

"Oh, girls, I need your help," said Robyn, clasping her hands together. "Jack Frost has stolen my magical objects and I have to find them quickly, or else all Christmas parties will be spoiled!"

Rachel and Kirsty exchanged a worried glance.

"What do you mean?" Rachel asked.

"I make sure that Christmas parties around the human and fairy worlds go well," Robyn explained. "Without them, all the parties will be ruined."

"That's terrible!" said Kirsty. "We have a party here later and everyone's been working really hard to get everything ready. It'd be awful for it to go wrong."

"We're having a Christmas Eve party in Fairyland tonight too," said Robyn.

"There will be special performances from lots of amazing fairies."

"Wasn't Jack Frost invited?" asked Rachel. "Is that why he stole your magical objects?"

"No, he was invited," said Robyn. "But we didn't put his Gobolicious Band on the performance list, and he was very cross."

"What are your magical objects?" Rachel asked.

"The magical cracker symbolises sharing, happiness and feasting," said Robyn. "It makes sure that there's plenty to eat and drink. The dancing shoes keep the party entertainment fun and exciting, and the snowglobe brings the Christmas party spirit to every gathering."

"We will help you before it's too late,"

said Kirsty in a determined voice.

"That's what I hoped you'd say," said Robyn, smiling. "If you come with me now, I can show you what Jack Frost has done in Fairyland."

Rachel and Kirsty nodded. They knew that Robyn's magic would make sure no one in the human world noticed they were gone, however long they spent in Fairyland.

Robyn gave a twirl and her silky dress floated out around her as she raised her wand.

Then she said:

We wish to be in Fairyland
To see the party being planned.
We have to stop Jack Frost today
So take us there without delay.

A shower of tiny golden sparkles sprinkled over the girls, and they felt themselves shrinking. Wings unfurled from their shoulders, and they fluttered into the air beside Robyn.

Then there was a bright flash of light,
and all at once they were standing at
the edge of a round ice rink, surrounded
by a glade of snowy fir trees. Imogen
the Ice Dance Fairy and Isla the Ice
Star Fairy were pirouetting around the
beautiful ice rink.

Rachel, Kirsty and Robyn had arrived
in Fairyland!

Jack Frost
on Ice

Rachel and Kirsty waved to their friends, and Imogen and Isla waved and skated over to them.

"Rachel! Kirsty!" said Isla in an excited voice. "It's great to see you! Are you here to help Robyn?"

"Yes," said Rachel. "It sounds like Jack Frost has been causing a lot of trouble."

"Without Robyn's magical objects, our performances might not go ahead," said Imogen sadly.

"Keep practising," said Kirsty, kindly. "We're not going to let Jack Frost spoil your party."

Robyn took the girls' hands.

"Look over there," she said.

Among the fir trees the girls

could see the jumbled pieces of a broken round stage. Behind it, a group of fairies were pointing their wands at a tall Christmas tree. It seemed to be growing taller and taller.

"The Christmas Fairies have been planning this party all year," said

Robyn. "That's a magical tree that was supposed to tower over the stage. We've been working on spells to make it grow its own decorations and gifts."

"It sounds amazing!" Rachel smiled.

"But we really have to stop Jack Frost," Robyn said, flicking back her long brown hair. "Let me show you what he did earlier today."

Robyn waved her wand over the ice rink, and the frozen surface became glassy. Then pictures appeared in the ice. The girls saw Jack Frost marching into the glade. His cloak swirled around him, and three scary-looking goblins scuttled along behind him.

Robyn was standing by the stage, watching the Dance Fairies practise their routine.

"I'll make you sorry for not putting my amazing Gobolicious Band in the show!"

Jack Frost yelled. "You stupid fairies
always think you can get your own way,
but I'm going to have the best Christmas
party in Fairyland – and your party is
going to FLOP!"

"Why do you have to be so mean?"
asked Robyn. "We've
been planning
this party for
months."

She picked
up a bag
that had
been sitting
at her feet.
Jack Frost
looked as if he
was going to explode with anger.

"I can do anything I like!" he

bellowed. "Especially with the help of a
bit of fairy magic!"

He pointed his wand at the bag
in Robyn's hands and a bolt of blue
lightning seemed to reach out and snatch
it. Robyn screamed and tried to hold
onto it, but Jack Frost's magic was
too strong.

He laughed loudly as the bag landed
in his hands.

"Those things are mine!" cried Robyn.

"I need them!"

"WRONG!" Jack Frost shouted. "*I* need them! But until I'm ready to use them, I'm going to hide them somewhere so clever that you stupid fairies will never find them!"

He handed the bag to the three goblins. Then he pointed his wand at them and chanted:

I know a Norwegian who likes to play pranks.

If he'll help trick the fairies I'll give him my thanks.

Tiaras and tutus conceal a great prize,

And keep it away from those bright fairy eyes.

The treasure will lie in a Christmassy nook.

33

The very last place a fairy would look.

When Jack Frost spoke the last word, the bag and the goblins disappeared in a blinding flash. The same lightning bolt hit the stage and smashed it into pieces.

Then the picture in the ice rink melted away, and Kirsty murmured the words of Jack Frost's spell under her breath.

"Have you got an idea?" Rachel asked her straight away.

"I think that Jack Frost was being too clever for his own good," said Kirsty. "He used that spell to hide Robyn's magical objects, right?"

"Right," said Robyn and Rachel together.

"So the spell holds the clues that will tell us where he hid the objects," said

Kirsty. "We just have to work out what the words mean."

"But how are we going to do that?" asked Robyn.

Kirsty gave a little smile. "I think I might know where to start," she said.

The Cottage in the Forest

"At school we've been learning about different Christmas traditions around the world," Kirsty explained. "The first part of Jack Frost's spell said something about a Norwegian, didn't it?"

"Yes," said Robyn, repeating the words out loud.

I know a Norwegian who likes to play pranks.

If he'll help trick the fairies I'll give him my thanks.

"I think in Norway there's a cheeky elf who plays tricks on people at Christmas," said Kirsty. "He looks after the animals on farms, as long as the farmers leave him bowls of porridge and the leftovers from the Christmas meal. If they don't leave him food, he causes trouble for them."

"I know him!" Robyn exclaimed. "He's called the Barn Elf."

"Robyn, can you take us to him?" asked Rachel.

Robyn nodded. "He lives in a distant part of Fairyland," she said. "It will take us a little while to fly there."

"Then let's get started," said Rachel. "We've got no time to waste!"

Soon the girls were flying beside Robyn, high above the green meadows of Fairyland. Slowly the toadstool houses and neat pathways gave way to heather-covered moorland and fields filled with wildflowers.

After what felt like a long time, Robyn
pointed to a dark-green forest just
below them.

"We'll have to go in there," she said.
"The Barn Elf lives in the middle of the
Magic Forest."

They swooped down and darted in
between the tall, straight tree trunks. In
the forest, it seemed
as dark as night.
Very little light
could filter through
the thick leaves.

"We've never
been to this part
of Fairyland
before," said Kirsty,
looking around as
they flew along.

There were no fairies fluttering around here. Suddenly Kirsty saw a pair of enormous eyes blinking right at her from behind a big branch.

"Don't be scared," said Robyn. "There are lots of magical creatures in this forest, but they only live here because they're shy."

A pink-coloured plume of smoke coiled under their noses, and the girls smelled a wonderful aroma.

"Mmm, it smells like coffee and toast," said Rachel.

"There are all sorts of mysterious magic in this forest," said Robyn.

"Listen!" said Kirsty.

From a clearing up ahead, they could hear a gruff voice humming a folk tune. Robyn gave a little smile.

"That's the Barn Elf," she said.

The three friends fluttered slowly to the forest floor. Old leaves crackled under their feet as they landed in the clearing.

A neat garden surrounded a small, white cottage with a red roof. A ladder was leaning against the side of the house, and there was a bucket at the foot of it.

"The humming's coming from the other side of the house," said Rachel. "Come on, let's fly around."

The friends flew around to the back of the house. The back door was open, leading into a cosy-looking kitchen.

A small elf was standing on the back doorstep, sipping a hot drink from a ceramic mug and rubbing the small of his back with one hand. He had a long white beard that reached almost to his feet, and he was wearing grey trousers and a grey tunic top. The only colourful thing about him was his bright-red hat. Rachel and Kirsty smiled at him, and saw that his beady eyes were sparkling and sharp.

"Well, well, well," he said. "What brings three little fairies all the way to the Magic Forest?"

"Hello, Barn Elf," said Robyn, hovering in front of him. "We came here looking for you."

The Barn Elf raised his eyebrows, and his beard twitched as if he was waggling his chin.

"How surprising!" he said. "What could the fairies want from me?"

"We were wondering if Jack Frost came to see you, and if you know anything about the magical objects he has stolen from Robyn," said Kirsty.

The Barn Elf paused as if he was thinking hard, and the girls thought that his eyes seemed to twinkle even more brightly.

"Jack Frost, eh?" he asked. "Well now, not meaning to be rude, but why should I tell you what you want to know?"

Despite his words he sounded friendly, and the girls were taken aback.

"Out of the goodness of your heart?" Kirsty suggested. "Robyn really needs your help."

The Barn Elf chuckled.

"I'm not loyal to anyone," he said. "But I sometimes give Jack Frost a helping hand. You see, I like pranks and tricks. And Jack Frost's very good at mischief. But King Oberon and Queen Titania of Fairyland don't like mischief as much as I do."

"But this isn't just mischief," Rachel pleaded. "Without Robyn's magical objects, the Fairyland Christmas party will be spoiled. If you know anything, please help us."

The Barn Elf swigged down the last of his drink and groaned as he gave the small of his back another rub.

"It makes no difference to me if the fairy party goes ahead or not," he said. "If you need something from me, you'll have to think of a way to make me *want* to help you."

"How can we do that?" Robyn asked.

The Barn Elf chuckled again.

"That's for you to work out!" he said.

The Cracker Hunt

Kirsty and Robyn looked at each other gloomily. It seemed as if the Barn Elf was determined not to help them. But Rachel kept watching him, and she saw him rub his back again.

"Have you hurt yourself?" she asked, feeling sorry for him.

"I've been cleaning the cottage windows," said the Barn Elf. "But I strained my poor old back when I was reaching up."

Rachel remembered seeing the ladder and the bucket at the front of the cottage. Suddenly, she had an idea.

"If we clean the windows for you, will you tell us what you know about Robyn's magical objects?" she asked.

The Barn Elf smiled.

"Now that is what I call fair," he said. "It's a deal. But only on the condition that you don't use magic to clean them."

Robyn waved her wand and gave each of them some small cloths and a bucket full of hot soapy water. They flew around the cottage and washed all the glass. Then they polished the windows

until they sparkled like diamonds. The
Barn Elf sat on a three-legged wooden
stool and watched them work with a
smile on his face.

When they had finished he nodded his
head and beckoned to them. Robyn
made the buckets and cloths vanish with
one flick of her magic wand, and they
flew down and landed in front of the
Barn Elf.

"Thank you," he said. "You've saved me a hard job. In return, I'll tell you what I know. Earlier today, a cracker arrived here in the post. It was addressed to Jack Frost, care of the Barn Elf."

"That must be my magical cracker!" Robyn exclaimed.

"I bet Jack Frost sent it here hoping that you would keep it safe," said Kirsty.

"That's what I thought," said the Barn Elf, nodding his head. "But as I explained, I'm not loyal to anyone. I don't obey the fairies and I don't obey Jack Frost."

"So may we have the cracker back?" asked Rachel.

The Barn Elf looked at her, his eyes gleaming with mischief.

"I only promised to tell you what I

knew," he said. "But I'm very glad to have my windows clean, so if you can find the cracker, you can keep it."

The three fairy friends exchanged determined glances.

"May we search your lovely cottage?" asked Robyn.

"Be my guests," chuckled the Barn Elf.

A great hunt began! The fairies fluttered, darted and zoomed through the rooms of the little cottage. They peered under cushions, opened cupboards and crept behind furniture, but it was no good.

The cracker was nowhere to be seen.

At last they returned to the sitting room and sat down in front of the fire.

It was a warm, Christmassy room with a glimmering tree, foil decorations looped along the walls and a stocking hanging over the cosy fireplace. The table in the corner was laid ready for Christmas dinner.

"Perhaps it's not in the cottage at all,"

said Robyn. "He could have hidden it anywhere in the forest."

"Or he could be carrying it right now," Kirsty suggested.

But Rachel shook her head.

"I don't think he would have left it in the forest," she said. "And his clothes don't have any pockets. I'm sure it's here, but he's wily. He's hidden it somewhere very clever."

"Yes," said Robyn, sounding baffled. "Jack Frost's spell talked about hiding things in a Christmassy nook. Perhaps it's tucked in a small cubbyhole somewhere and we'll never find it."

"We'll find it," said Rachel, squeezing the fairy's hand.

The girls thought hard. Then Kirsty gave a little laugh.

"Where's the best place to hide something?" she asked. "Among lots of other things that are just the same! And where do you find lots of crackers?"

"On the dining table!" shouted Robyn and Rachel together.

The three of them zoomed over to the Barn Elf's little dining table. There was a box of six crackers on the end of the table. Five of them looked exactly the same, but the sixth cracker was pink and yellow, and was

glittering with sparkles of fairy dust.

"My magical cracker!" Robyn exclaimed. "We've found it!"

She picked it up and it instantly shrank to fairy-size. The girls quickly flew out of the cottage and found the Barn Elf still sitting on his little stool. He smiled when he saw Robyn holding her magical cracker.

"Well found," he said.

"It was a good hiding place," said Kirsty. "It was fun trying to find it!"

"It's been very interesting to meet you all," replied the Barn Elf. "I shall have to thank Jack Frost for arranging it."

He chuckled again, and Robyn turned to the girls.

"You've been wonderful," she said. "I'm going to send you home now, because I have to return my magical cracker to its rightful place. But I'll come and get you later to look for the other objects, if that's okay?"

Kirsty and Rachel exchanged a happy glance.

"Of course," said Rachel. "One down, two to go!"

The Dancing Shoes

Contents

Party Plans

Rachel and Kirsty returned to
Wetherbury in a swirl of fairy dust.
Thanks to Robyn's magic, no time had
passed in the human world while they
had been away. They crept out from
under the table where they had been
hiding, and quickly finished putting the
crackers on the place settings.

"No more crackers are going off by themselves, thank goodness," said Rachel with a smile.

"Yes, and all the problems with the Christmas decorations seem to be fixed," Kirsty added, looking around the hall. "It must be because we found Robyn's magical cracker."

Mrs Tate walked over to the girls.

"The tables look beautiful," she said. "Well done!"

"What else can we do to help?" asked Rachel happily.

"There are still lots of decorations to put up," Mrs Walker replied. "Then the Christmas tree needs to be dressed and the balloons have to be blown up."

Rachel glanced up at the clock on the wall. It was almost lunchtime.

"We'd better get started!" she said.

The girls worked hard. They put baubles and lights on the tree, hung paper chains across the room, and then started to blow up the balloons. They only stopped for five minutes to eat the sandwiches that Mrs Tate had made. Neither of them had a moment to think about Robyn or Jack Frost's spell.

At three o'clock, Kirsty tied the neck
of the last balloon and, then let out a
long breath.

"I think we must have blown up
hundreds of balloons," she said.

"I definitely think we've done enough,"
said Rachel, giggling.

The hall floor could hardly be seen
under all the bouncing balloons.

"I don't know what
we'd have done
without you two,"
said Mrs Tate,
looking around.

"Can we do
anything else,
Mum?" Kirsty
asked.

"Well, the ballet
dancers are busy rehearsing in the side
room," said Mrs Tate, pointing to a
closed door. "Why don't you take a
break and watch the dancing? I might
join you in a little while."

The girls nodded eagerly. The
highlight of the party was going to be
a performance of the famous Christmas
party scene from *The Nutcracker*. The

two friends loved ballet and they couldn't
wait to see it.

Rachel and Kirsty knocked on the
side room door and went in. The room
was filled with dancers in frilly, frothy
costumes. The beautiful *Nutcracker*
music was playing in the background,
and the director was standing in the
middle of the room. He was clutching his
hair with both hands.

Behind the dancers, the girls could see
boxes wrapped up to look like presents,
a nutcracker doll and a little white
jewellery box.

"That's the doll that magically comes
to life in the ballet," said Rachel,
pointing to the nutcracker doll.

The girls smiled at each other. They
knew all about magic, thanks to their

friendship with the fairies.

Just then, one of the dancers fell over and three other ballerinas stumbled over her. The music stopped.

"No, no, NO!" the director exclaimed. "You all knew these steps perfectly yesterday. What's the matter with you?"

The dancers gathered around the director and started arguing and trying to explain.

"It doesn't sound as if rehearsals are going very well," said Kirsty.

"It must be because Robyn's dancing shoes are missing," said Rachel. "We *have* to get them back before the performance starts this afternoon."

"That means we have to solve the next part of Jack Frost's spell," Kirsty added. "If we don't, the fairy party will be ruined too."

The girls had already solved the first two lines of the spell, but there were still four lines to understand.

Suddenly, Rachel noticed something. The lid of the little jewellery box was open, and music had begun to tinkle.

"Look, there's a tiny ballerina inside that jewellery box," she said.

Kirsty looked and then gave a big smile.

"That's not a ballerina, Rachel," she said. "That's Robyn!"

Mystery Ballerina

Robyn pirouetted into the air and
zoomed towards the girls. She flew high
over the heads of the dancers, but luckily
none of them looked up. They were too
busy panicking about the performance.

"Hello, Rachel and Kirsty," Robyn
said in an excited voice. "I came because
I think the next part of the spell might
have something to do with the dance at
your party. It's a ballet, isn't it?"

"Yes," said Rachel. "What are the words again?"

Robyn recited:

"Tiaras and tutus conceal a great prize,
And keep it away from those bright fairy eyes."

"The rehearsals aren't going very well," said Kirsty, pointing to the arguing dancers. "I wonder if Jack Frost has hidden the dancing shoes here!"

"Time's running out," said Robyn.

"If the magic dancing shoes are here, we have to find them soon. Without them, all Christmas party entertainments will be ruined."

"It would be easier to look around if we were fairies," Rachel smiled, looking at Robyn.

Robyn winked and in an instant the girls were fluttering in the air beside her on gauzy wings. The three friends split up and flew around the room, keeping an eye on the dancers to make sure that no one spotted them.

A few minutes
later they met
up again
behind the
jewellery
box.

"Any luck?"
asked Robyn.

"I saw lots of
sweet wrappers dropped on the floor
over there," said Kirsty, pointing. "The
dancers aren't litterbugs. Do you think it
could be a goblin?"

"They do like sweets," Robyn agreed.
"And Jack Frost might have told a goblin
to guard the dancing shoes."

"One of the dancers has lost her tutu,"
Rachel added. "I overheard her telling
the others about it."

Just then, the music started again. The director clapped his hands together.

"Places, everyone!" he called. "Let's start from the beginning."

The dancers all hurried to their positions and the scene began again.

Robyn and the girls fluttered behind a curtain to watch. But once again, the dancers forgot the steps.

"Hopeless!" roared the director. "Absolutely hopeless! And the only dancer who's remembered all the steps is dressed completely wrong. Why are you wearing green tights?"

The girls exchanged surprised glances and peeped around the curtain. At the end of a row of dancers was a short ballerina in a frothy pink tutu.

She had green, bandy legs and a pointy
nose, but her dance steps were perfect.

"Oh my goodness," whispered Kirsty.
"It's a goblin!"

Disaster on the Dance Floor

"Yes, and he's got my dancing shoes,"
Robyn added. "Look!"

A tiny pair of silver ballet shoes was
hanging around the goblin's neck on a
little chain.

"He's turned them into a charm," said
Rachel in a worried voice.

"That's why he can dance so well," said Robyn with a heavy sigh. "The magic of my dancing shoes is giving him all the talent."

They watched the goblin ballerina perform an elegant leap across the room. The director clapped his hands together.

"Everyone, look at this! That's what you should all be doing!" he cried.

The goblin ballerina was soon hidden among a crowd of other dancers, who were trying to copy his steps.

"How are we going to get the dancing shoes away from him?" asked Kirsty.

Suddenly Rachel gave a little smile and pointed across the rehearsal room.

"Someone else is trying to reach him too," she said.

A plump goblin was hopping around the edge of the room, trying to talk to his goblin friend while hidding from the ballet dancers at the same time.

"Let's fly nearer to him," Kirsty suggested.

"Perhaps we can get closer to the other goblin by following him."

The three friends flew down and hovered behind the plump goblin. They could hear him muttering to himself.

"Why is he messing around with these stupid dancers?" the goblin grumbled. "We have to get to the Ice Castle as quickly as possible or Jack Frost won't be able to put on his dance competition."

"Did you hear that?" whispered
Rachel. "Jack Frost wants to use
the dancing shoes for his own dance
competition. We have to stop the goblins
taking them away!"

Just then, the music stopped again.

"It's a dance disaster!" cried the
director. "This is all wrong! Start again!"

Kirsty pulled Rachel and Robyn
behind the nearest curtain. She turned to
Robyn with sparkling eyes.

"Robyn, can you turn us into
ballerinas?" she asked with a smile. "I've
got an idea!"

Robyn waved her wand, and instantly
Rachel and Kirsty were transformed
back to human-size. They stepped out
from behind the curtain and looked at
each other. Rachel was wearing a red

silk tutu, and Kirsty's outfit was made of yellow satin. Their hair was held up in buns with matching ribbons tied around them. Robyn hid herself in a fold of Rachel's tutu.

"These would be the best party dresses ever!" Rachel exclaimed.

"Come on," said Kirsty. "I think that this is the only way to get close to the goblin ballerina. We have to dance!"

Pirouette Pile-up

Feeling very nervous, Rachel and Kirsty slipped in among the other dancers. Everyone was talking at once, and no one even noticed the two new ballerinas. Kirsty's heart was thumping so loudly she thought that everyone must be able to hear it.

"Come on," said Rachel, taking Kirsty's hand. "Let's find that goblin!"

She pulled her best friend through the crowd of dancers until they reached the goblin ballerina. He was standing on one big toe. His other leg stretched out behind him, and a tiara was hanging crookedly over one ear.

"He might recognise us," Kirsty whispered. "We've met a lot of Jack Frost's goblins."

There was a small group of dancers to the right of the goblin. Rachel led Kirsty to the back of the group, keeping out of the goblin's view.

"If we can dance up behind him, we might be able to lift the charm from around his neck," said Kirsty.

"Places, please!" called the director, clapping his hands. "Hurry! We don't have long!"

The beautiful music began to play again, and all the ballerinas took up their positions. Rachel and Kirsty each chose a dancer and tried to copy her movements. But the dancers kept tripping up and turning the wrong way. They stumbled over their own feet and landed with loud thumps instead of graceful steps. Soon the director was pulling on his own hair again.

"You sound like a herd of elephants!" he complained.

The goblin pirouetted past the girls,

and the charm swung out towards Kirsty.
She reached out to try to grab it, but the
goblin had already twirled away.

"Arms up, and smile!" ordered the
director. "This is a Christmas party
scene, so you're all supposed to be
dancing and looking happy."

The goblin gave a wide grin that
looked more like a grimace. He whirled
past Rachel, and she saw the dancing

shoes charm shining on the chain. Her heart thumped as she reached her hand towards the charm. She felt it brush her fingertips, but she couldn't hold onto it and it flew past.

The girls danced on, following the other dancers as well as they could. But they kept tripping over their own feet.

"I'm being so clumsy!" Kirsty cried.

"It's because that greedy goblin ballerina is using all the magic of the dancing shoes for himself," Robyn whispered, looking up at her from the folds of Rachel's tutu netting.

Rachel stubbed her toe against a table.

"We have to get the charm back," she cried, "or the dance will be a disaster."

The girls tried their best, but every time the goblin came close to them, the charm slipped out of their grasp. As the dance went on, Kirsty saw the door of the rehearsal room open. Then Mrs Tate put her head around the door.

"Kirsty, it's your mum!" Rachel said in a low voice. "She must have come to watch the rehearsal!"

"But if she sees us dancing she's bound to say something," Kirsty gasped.

In her panic, she stopped dancing.

97

Suddenly two other dancers crashed
into her and they all tumbled down in
a heap. The goblin was mid-pirouette,
and he squawked as he toppled sideways
over the other dancers. Within a few
seconds there was a pile of dancers in the
middle of the room, with the goblin at
the bottom.

Kirsty found herself squashed up against the goblin's smelly feet!

"Help!" she said, coughing and holding her nose. "Rachel! Please help me out!"

A Safe Pair of Shoes!

Kirsty wriggled and jiggled as hard as she could. Then she felt Rachel's hands grasping hers.

"Pull!" whispered Rachel.

As Kirsty was sliding out from underneath the pile of dancers, she spotted something silvery out of the corner of her eye. It was half hidden under a tutu, but it glinted in the light.

"Rachel!" Kirsty exclaimed. "I can see the chain!"

Kirsty lunged for the chain just as the goblin squirmed around and spotted her.

"My charm!" he squawked. "Get off it!"

His long fingers scrabbled towards the chain.

Kirsty stretched out her arm to try to reach it first. Then the plump goblin stuck his head into the pile between them.

"What's going on?" he snapped. "We have to get to the Ice Castle *now!*"

"I'm trapped!" wailed the ballerina goblin. "And I've dropped the magic charm necklace!"

"You idiot!" snarled the plump goblin. "Look, those pesky girls are trying to get it before us."

"Quick, Kirsty!" cried Rachel.

With a determined stretch, Kirsty got her fingers to the chain at exactly the same moment as the plump goblin. They each grabbed it and pulled – and the dancing shoes flew off the chain and into the air!

Rachel caught them in one hand and tugged Kirsty out of the pile of dancers with the other. Then she looked up and saw Mrs Tate heading their way.

"Your mum's coming over!" said Rachel. "Come on!"

The girls darted behind the curtain and Robyn flew out of Rachel's tutu. Kirsty handed her the dancing shoes.

"Thank you so much!" said the little fairy. "You're wonderful friends." Tears of happiness sparkled in her eyes as the dancing shoes

returned to their proper size. With two
taps of Robyn's wand, Rachel and Kirsty
were back in their ordinary clothes. They
hugged each other in excitement.

"Hurray!
We did it!"
said Kirsty
in delight.

"You were
both amazing,"
said Robyn.
"I must take
the dancing shoes
back to Fairyland
now, but I'll be back
really soon. I still have to find my
snowglobe before the parties start, and I
know I can't do it without you two."

She blew a kiss to each of the girls.

Then she disappeared in a little puff of
fairy dust. Kirsty nudged Rachel and
they watched as the two goblins trudged
out of the room, elbowing each other
and scowling. One of them was still
wearing his crooked tiara.

The girls shared a smile and slipped out from behind the curtain to join Mrs Tate.

"Oh, hello, girls!" she said, hugging them. "I was so worried about the rehearsals that I didn't see you."

"It looks as if things are going better now," said Rachel happily.

The ballerinas were dancing beautifully, and the director was smiling.

"I wonder what Jack Frost will say when he finds out that Robyn has two of her magical objects back," said Rachel in a low voice.

"I don't care what he says," said Kirsty.
"I'm just happy that all performances at
Christmas parties are now safe."

"I can't wait to see the ballet later,"
Rachel giggled.

Kirsty put her arm around her best
friend and grinned at her.

"Me neither," she said. "It's going to
be magical!"

The Snowglobe

Contents

An Exciting Idea

"We're finally ready for the party!" said Kirsty, looking around the Town Hall.

The tables were laden with delicious food, the tree was bright with lights and baubles, and foil decorations were looped across the ceiling. Mrs Tate pulled aside the curtains and peered out of the window. Then she turned to Rachel and Kirsty with a smile.

"The stars are out, the snow is falling and Father Christmas has set out in his sleigh," she said.

"*And* it's time for the party to start!" added Rachel in delight, giving a little skip of excitement.

She and Kirsty had worked very hard to help get ready for Wetherbury's Christmas party.

"I just hope that we have enough time to find Robyn's magical snowglobe," Kirsty whispered.

They had found two of the three items that Jack Frost had stolen, but without her snowglobe, Robyn would not be able to make sure that Christmas parties were full of the Christmas party spirit. Jack Frost's mysterious spell held the clue to where they would find the globe. But so far they hadn't been able to work it out. Rachel and Kirsty were a little worried, but for now all they could think about was the party.

"It all starts in the town square," said Mrs Tate, pulling on her coat.

"The carol singers are going to lead the procession from the clock tower, through the town and back here for the party. We'd better hurry up if we want to join them at the start!"

The girls eagerly wrapped up in their coats, hats, scarves and gloves. Then they hurried out to join the procession.

A crowd of people was watching the carol singers underneath the clock tower.

Each of them was
holding a lantern
or a carol sheet,
and they were
singing 'Away
In A Manger'.
A small band of
musicians played
behind them,
their instruments
shining in the
lantern light.

The snow was falling gently, and the girls drew in their breath.

"It's so pretty!" said Rachel in a happy voice.

But just as she spoke, a gust of wind blew out one of the lanterns…then another…then another.

As the singers scrabbled to relight their lanterns, the girls heard confused cries from some of the others.

"Where's my carol sheet?"

"Mine's gone missing too!"

"I've lost the order of songs – what comes next?"

Suddenly the trumpet let out a strange parping sound, and the girls heard muffled laughter from the crowd.

"This is all because Jack Frost still has the snowglobe," whispered Kirsty. "If things keep going wrong, this party will turn into a joke."

"The procession is about to set off," said Rachel. "Oh, Kirsty, we have to find the snowglobe before everyone reaches the Town Hall. Otherwise, Jack Frost will ruin our party!"

The procession made its way out of the town square, and the girls stayed near the back, thinking hard. Mrs Tate was chatting to some friends nearby. When the procession reached the high street, Rachel gave Kirsty's hand a squeeze.

"I've thought of something," she said. "Jack Frost's spell says that the snowglobe is hidden 'where pesky fairies won't think to look', remember?"

Kirsty nodded, looking interested.

"I was just thinking about how the Barn Elf hid the magical cracker in such an obvious place that we almost didn't think to look there," Rachel went on. "So where is the very last place that the fairies would look for something that was stolen *from* the magical glade? *In* the magical glade, of course!"

Kirsty's eyes opened very wide.

"I think you've solved it!" she cried.
"Oh, Rachel, we have to get to
Fairyland straight away!"

A Search in Fairyland

After one of their first adventures with
the fairies, Queen Titania had given the
girls a wonderful present. They each had
a special locket filled with fairy dust.
If they ever needed to see the fairies
urgently, all they had to do was open
the lockets and sprinkle some fairy dust
over themselves. They would instantly
transform into fairies and be whisked

away to Fairyland. There was just one tiny problem…

"How are we going to use our magic lockets without anyone seeing us?" Kirsty groaned.

The high street was filled with people following the procession, and Mrs Tate kept turning around to check on them. Rachel looked around and frowned. All the shops were shut, and there were no handy alleyways to dart into while they transformed. They walked on, looking left and right to try to find somewhere they could hide.

Suddenly there was a loud, clanging CRASH at the front of the procession. One of the musicians had dropped an instrument.

As people hurried forward to see what

was happening, Kirsty quickly grabbed
Rachel's arm.

"It's now or never!" she exclaimed.
"Everyone's looking at the musician.
Let's go!"

The girls opened their lockets and
sprinkled the sparkling fairy dust over
themselves. Instantly,
they shrank to
fairy-size and
felt gossamer
wings
unfurling on
their backs.
Then there
was a golden
flash, and they
were standing in a
snowy glade in Fairyland.

They saw Robyn immediately. She was standing beside the broken stage with Natalie the Christmas Stocking Fairy and Chrissie the Wish Fairy. They all looked very serious.

"Robyn! Natalie! Chrissie!" called Rachel, waving to them.

She and Kirsty landed beside the fairies. They hugged Natalie and Chrissie.

"It's lovely to see you again," Kirsty exclaimed.

"All the Christmas Fairies are here," said Robyn with a smile.

She waved her hand towards the ice-skating rink. The girls could see Holly and Cheryl chatting to Paige, Stella, Gabriella and Angelica.

"We were supposed to be putting the finishing touches to the glade," said Chrissie, giving a helpless shrug. "But we've had to stop – none of our spells are working properly."

"Rachel's had an idea," said Kirsty.

Together, the girls explained why they thought that the snowglobe might be hidden in the glade. The fairies were excited by the idea.

"But if the snowglobe *is* here, shouldn't it have mended the broken stage by now?" asked Rachel.

"I don't think so," said Robyn. "The snowglobe's magic obeys the wishes of whoever is holding it."

"So the goblin who is guarding it for
Jack Frost is stopping its magic from
mending the broken stage and everything
else?" said Kirsty.

"Exactly," said Robyn. "So it's
definitely worth a try!"

Rachel, Kirsty and the Christmas
Fairies started to search.
They looked behind
bushes, around the
ice rink and in
every shadowy
nook and cranny
of the glade.
They even flew
up into the trees in
case the goblin had
scrambled up there.

But there was no sign of a goblin or of the snowglobe.

Rachel fluttered down and sat on a piece of the broken stage, and Robyn and Kirsty joined her. Rachel rested her chin on her hand and sighed.

"Perhaps I made a mistake about the meaning of the spell," she said. "I probably got it all wrong."

Robyn patted Rachel kindly on the shoulder.

"I still think your idea made sense," she said. "Don't be upset, Rachel. You and Kirsty have been helping me so much. But we've searched everywhere."

Just then, Kirsty gave a little squeak of excitement.

"There's one place we haven't checked!" she said, waving her hand around at the pieces of rubble. "*Under the broken stage!*"

A Pinch
of Pepper

The fairies looked at each other in
excitement. Suddenly they all felt
absolutely certain that the goblin was
somewhere under the stage. They got
down on their hands and knees and
peered into the dark spaces between
the broken stage sections. But they still
couldn't see anything.

Robyn took out her wand and pointed it into the darkness.

"Sneeze and sniffle, head to toes.
Let my spell get up your nose!"

A thin stream of something black and powdery shot out of the wand tip and into the darkness.

"What is that?" asked Kirsty.

"Pepper," Robyn whispered, winking at them over her shoulder.

She put her finger to her lips and then flew up and hovered over the centre of the stage. Hardly daring to breathe or move, the girls listened. Seconds ticked past and they heard nothing. Then…

"ACHOOOOOOOOOO!"

"He's here!" Rachel exclaimed, leaping to her feet. "We've found him!"

Robyn flew back to them and they all shared a hug.

"We've done it!" cried Robyn, jumping up and down with excitement. "We've found my magical snowglobe!"

"Yes," said Kirsty, "but how are we going to get it back?"

They looked at the stage and realised how clever Jack Frost had been. They couldn't mend it without the snowglobe, but they couldn't reach the snowglobe until the stage was mended.

"We need to be even smaller than fairies to get in there," said Rachel. "Robyn, can you make us really tiny? Maybe we can persuade the goblin to give back the snowglobe."

Robyn waved her wand in a circle around them. A shimmering band of golden light appeared for a moment, and then they shrank until they were no bigger than fireflies.

Suddenly the stage seemed easy to access. There were wide gaps between the floorboards, and the three friends swooped through to the dark foundations of the stage. They flitted around bits of broken wood and between heavy blocks. There was a strong smell of damp earth, and they could feel little bursts of icy air coming from all directions.

"Stop!" whispered Kirsty, who was flying ahead. "I can see the goblin!"

He was sitting hunched up with his back against a wonky wooden post. His teeth were chattering loudly, and a drip from his nose had frozen into a tiny icicle. He was gazing down at his bony hands.

"Let's fly around behind him and see if we can spot the snowglobe," Robyn suggested softly.

Keeping in the shadows, they flew carefully around the goblin until they were hovering behind his earlobe. There

was nothing on the ground at his side,
but then Rachel looked over his shoulder
and beckoned to the others. Without
saying a word, she pointed down at
his hands.

The goblin
was clasping
a beautiful
crystal
globe, set
on a silver
base. Tiny
flakes of
snow whirled
around the

miniature Christmas tree. The star on top
of the tree seemed to give out real light,
and as the snow swirled around it, the
globe seemed to sparkle even more. The

goblin couldn't take his eyes off it.

"The snowglobe is enormous now that we're so small," whispered Robyn. "Even if we could distract him from it, there's no way we could lift it."

"Then we'll have to persuade him to come out and give it to us," said Rachel in a firm voice. "Come on!"

Butterfingers!

Rachel flew out to hover in front of the goblin's face, and Kirsty and Robyn zoomed after her.

"Excuse me, goblin," said Rachel in a polite voice.

The goblin gave a start and bumped his head on the stage.

"Ow!" he groaned, scowling. "That was your fault, you stupid fairy!"

"That snowglobe doesn't belong to you," said Robyn.

"Who cares?" the goblin snapped, rubbing his knobbly head. "*I've* got it now."

"But you're spoiling all Christmas parties by keeping it here," said Kirsty. "And it doesn't look as if you're having much fun."

"It's cold, draughty and damp," said the goblin, glaring at her. "I love it!"

"Oh dear," said Rachel with a sigh. "Listen, goblin, it will soon be Christmas. Don't you want to do something kind for a change?"

The goblin's eyes opened wide and for a moment Rachel felt hopeful. But...

"NO!" he bellowed.

Rachel and Kirsty glanced at each other, looking sad.

"While we're under here, we're too small to be able to take the snowglobe back," Kirsty whispered. "We need to get the goblin back into the glade. Perhaps then we'll think of a way to get the snowglobe."

"But how are we going to get him out?" asked Rachel. "He says he likes it down here."

"Exactly!" Robyn exclaimed. "He says he likes it because it's cold and miserable – so let's change things a little!"

She waved her wand, and suddenly the icy blasts of wind stopped. Instead, the girls felt a warm breeze ruffle their hair, scented with apple blossom.

"PWORR!" grumbled the goblin. "What a pong!"

The air grew warmer and sweat began to pour down his face. Then all the broken slabs and bricks turned a delicate shade of pink, and pictures of fluffy kittens and puppies appeared on them.

"YUCK!" yelled the goblin. "What's happening? This is awful!"

Rachel and Kirsty covered their mouths, trying to stifle their giggles.

Finally, tinkling ballet music began to play, and the goblin leapt to his feet.

"I'm not staying here!" he wailed. "It's torment!"

He scrabbled his way past the broken blocks, shoving them out of his way and sending bricks and slabs flying in all directions. He burst out through a thin plank of wood and jumped on top of the rubble.

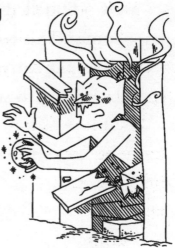

"Quick, follow him!" cried Kirsty.

The friends whizzed out through the gap that the goblin had made as fast as they could, and Robyn instantly returned them to fairy-size.

The goblin was scrambling and stumbling across the rubble of the stage. He was holding the snowglobe in one hand, but it kept half-slipping out of his grasp as he wobbled along.

"He's going to drop it!" gasped Robyn in a horrified voice. "If it smashes, Christmas parties will be spoiled forever!"

The three fairies fluttered around his head in a panic.

"Put the snowglobe down," Robyn pleaded.

"Leave me alone!" shouted the goblin.

"Just let us have the snowglobe!"
Rachel cried. "It belongs to Robyn."

Suddenly there was a blinding flash
of lightning, and Jack Frost appeared in
front of them.

"Where's my special snowglobe?" he
screeched angrily.

Shocked, the goblin flung his hands up
and the snowglobe flew into the air.

"NO!" yelled Kirsty and Rachel.

"BUTTERFINGERS!" cried Jack
Frost loudly.

"HELP!" the goblin squawked.

Robyn zoomed after the snowglobe,
which made an arc in the air and then
began to fall. Faster and faster it hurtled
towards the ground. Robyn raced across
the glade as the others held their breath.
Robyn dived for the snowglobe with her
hands outstretched…

"YES!" cheered Rachel and Kirsty.

The Christmas Party Fairy had caught her snowglobe in the nick of time! Jack Frost snarled and grabbed the goblin's ear with his fingertips.

"You numbskull!" he roared. "Now look what you've done!"

"It was those pesky fairies, Your Worshipfulness!" wailed the goblin.

"I'll get my revenge!" the Ice Lord declared angrily.

"Not this Christmas, Jack Frost!" said

Robyn, folding her arms across her chest.

Grumbling loudly, Jack Frost and the goblin disappeared in a flash of blue lightning. Robyn turned to the girls and held up the snowglobe with a beaming smile. It had returned to fairy-size, and it was giving out a warm, Christmassy glow. Robyn shook it, and it sparkled as the snow swirled.

"I wish for everything to return to normal," she said.

There was a loud whooshing sound,
and the pieces of rubble around them
started to tremble.

In a swirl of sparkles, they were
whisked up into the air – and replaced
on a stage that was as good as new!

"We did it!" Kirsty exclaimed, twirling into the air in delight. "Christmas parties are saved!"

"All thanks to you!" said Robyn, hugging the girls. "But it's getting late. We have to work fast to get everything ready for the party!"

Parties Galore!

Rachel, Kirsty and the Christmas Fairies worked very hard to make sure that the party would be perfect. When the guests arrived, the glade looked enchanting, with tiny sparkling lights in every tree and exquisitely wrapped presents hanging from the branches.

Rachel and Kirsty were thrilled to see so many familiar faces. The Rainbow Fairies swooped down to greet them with hugs and kisses. The Pet Keeper Fairies hurried over to say hello, and crowds of other fairy friends waved, blew kisses and wished them a happy Christmas.

The performances were wonderful. First there was superb ballroom, Latin and ballet dancing. Then there was a wonderful carol concert from the Music Fairies...and the goblins!

"My hands hurt from clapping so hard!" said Kirsty, taking a sip of her delicious blackberry-dew.

Rachel smiled and then gasped as a murmur went around the crowd of fairies. Jack Frost had walked into the glade!

"He looks cross," whispered Kirsty.

The fairies parted to let him through, and he stalked towards the stage. He was glaring at the goblins, whose knees started knocking together.

Robyn stepped into his path. With one hand she held up her snowglobe and shook it, and with her other hand she offered Jack Frost a mug of hot berry juice. A smile flickered around his thin lips, and he took the mug.

"That's the Christmas party spirit weaving its magic!" said Rachel.

Jack Frost sat down in a front-row seat as Imogen and Isla stepped onto the ice rink for the next performance. It was going to be a magnificent show.

Robyn's party was everything the perfect Christmas party should be. There was wonderful food, plenty of dancing and singing, and lots of laughter. At last, with streamers dangling from their hair and music ringing in their ears, it was time for the girls to go home. Robyn tapped their lockets with her wand to fill them with fairy dust again. Then she hugged them both tightly.

"Thank you for helping me to save Christmas parties everywhere," she said. "You're wonderful friends!"

"We're glad we could help," said
Rachel. "And thank you for inviting us
to an amazing party!"

"Yours is going to be just as amazing,"
said Robyn. "And it's time you were
there! Goodbye, girls, and Happy
Christmas!"

The sound of fairy laughter and music
was suddenly replaced by the voices of
the Wetherbury carol singers. The girls
were back in the human world, and not
a moment had passed since they had left.

Rachel and Kirsty were still at the back
of the procession, but now the lanterns
were all glittering and the musicians were
playing perfectly.

"Come on, girls, don't dawdle!" called
Mrs Tate, glancing back at them. "We're
nearly at the Town Hall!"

Everyone in Wetherbury agreed that it was the best Christmas party ever. The ballerinas had never danced so perfectly, the carol singers had never sounded so sweet, and the music had never been so tuneful. The party guests clapped and clapped, and the girls' hands ached from joining in, after all the applause at the fairy party earlier.

When everyone sat down to enjoy the feast, Kirsty and Rachel had fun trying all the different cakes, pies, sandwiches and puddings that filled the tables. They didn't even notice how late it was until the clock struck midnight. On the first BONG, the doors of the Town Hall flew wide open.

"Ho ho ho!" said a merry voice.

"It's Father Christmas!" said Kirsty in delight.

"And he's got a sackful of presents!" Rachel added with an excited giggle.

As Father Christmas made his way around the hall, handing out presents and shaking hands, Rachel turned to Kirsty and gave her a hug.

"Thank you for inviting me to spend Christmas with you," she said. "I love the adventures we have together!"

"Me too," said Kirsty, hugging her in return. "And I'm so lucky to have such an amazing best friend. Today has been the best Christmas Eve *ever!*"

Now **Kirsty and Rachel**
must help...

Mae the Panda Fairy

Read on for a sneak peek...

Kirsty Tate gazed happily at the tall
hedgerows, her bare arm resting on the
open window as the car travelled along
the bumpy country road. Pretty red,
yellow and pink flowers were tangled
among the green leaves. She could smell
the tang of cut grass and the earthiness
of freshly turned soil.

"We're nearly there, girls," said Mrs
Tate from the driver's seat. "Look!"

She slowed the car and pointed at a
signpost at the side of the winding road.
WILD WOODS NATURE RESERVE – 2 MILES

Kirsty smiled at her best friend Rachel Walker, who was sitting beside her.

"I'm so excited," said Rachel. "The sun's shining, we've got all of the summer holidays stretching out ahead of us, and a whole week to spend here at the reserve with the animals."

It was the start of the summer holidays, and Kirsty and Rachel were on their way to Wild Woods, the local nature reserve. Rachel was staying with Kirsty, and their parents had arranged for them to spend every day that week there as volunteers. As the car turned up a rough, narrow track, their hearts were racing with anticipation.

"It's going to be amazing to be helping out as junior rangers," said Kirsty. "I can't wait to see the animals!"

At the end of the track was an archway, printed with green words:

WELCOME TO WILD WOODS

NATURE RESERVE

Mrs Tate drove through the archway and stopped the car next to a small wooden hut. The door of the hut opened and a tanned, dark-haired woman came out. She was wearing khaki shorts, a white shirt and walking boots, and she waved at them with a smile.

"Look, there's Becky," said Mrs Tate. "She's the head of Wild Woods."

Rachel and Kirsty jumped out of the car and Becky walked over to them.

Read **Mae the Panda Fairy** to find out what adventures are in store for Kirsty and Rachel!

Meet the fairies, play games
and get sneak peeks at
the latest books!

www.rainbowmagicbooks.co.uk

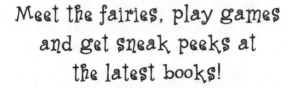

There's fairy fun for everyone on
our wonderful website.
You'll find great activities, competitions, stories and
fairy profiles, and also a special newsletter.

Get 30% off all Rainbow Magic books at
www.rainbowmagicbooks.co.uk

Enter the code RAINBOW at the checkout.
Offer ends 31 December 2013.

Offer valid in United Kingdom and Republic of Ireland only.

Meet the Sweet Fairies

If Kirsty and Rachel don't find
the Sweet Fairies' magical charms,
Jack Frost will ruin all sweet treats for ever!

www.rainbowmagicbooks.co.uk

Competition!

Robyn the Christmas Party Fairy has created this special crossword just for you! Read the clues and put the correct answers in the grid below. When you have all four answers, go online and enter the competition

CLUES

Down

1. What do people decorate in their homes at Christmas time?

_ _ _ _

3. What large bird do people traditionally eat on Christmas Day?

_ _ _ _ _ _

Across

2. One of Santa's reindeer has a bright red nose. What is his name?

_ _ _ _ _ _ _

4. What do you pull on Christmas Day that makes a loud noise?

_ _ _ _ _ _ _

We will put all the correct entries into a draw and select a winner to receive a special Rainbow Magic Goody Bag featuring lots of treats for you and your fairy friends.
You'll also star in a new Rainbow Magic story!

Enter online now at www.rainbowmagicbooks.co.uk

No purchase required. Only one entry per child.
One prize draw will take place on 31st March 2014 and June 30th 2014. Alternatively readers can send the four answers on a postcard to: Rainbow Magic, Robyn the Christmas Party Fairy Competition, Orchard Books, 338 Euston Road, London, NW1 3BH. Australian readers can write to: Rainbow Magic, Robyn the Christmas Party Fairy Competition, Hachette Children's Books, level 17/207 Kent St, Sydney, NSW 2000. E-mail: childrens.books@hachette.com.au. New Zealand readers should write to Rainbow Magic, Robyn the Christmas Party Fairy Competition, 4 Whetu Place, Mairangi Bay, Auckland, NZ

Meet the
Baby Animal Rescue
Fairies

The Baby Animal Rescue Fairies have lost all their magical items. But luckily, Kirsty and Rachel are there to save the day and make sure all baby animals in the world are safe and sound.

www.rainbowmagicbooks.co.uk